Published by Dial Books for Young Readers
A Division of Penguin USA Inc.
375 Hudson Street
New York, New York 10014

Copyright © 1990 by Yvonne Gilbert
Created and designed by Halcyon Books, Inc. and Yvonne Gilbert
Printed in Hong Kong by South China Printing Company (1988) Limited
E
First Edition
1 3 5 7 9 10 8 6 4 2

Library of Congress Cataloging in Publication Data
Baby's book of lullabies and cradle songs.
Summary: A collection of sixteen traditional lullabies
from around the world, including "Hush Little Baby,"
"Golden Slumbers," and "Little Red Bird."
1. Lullabies. [1. Lullabies. 2. Poetry—Collections]
I. Gilbert, Yvonne.
PN6109.97.B43 1990   782.42'15'23   89-25898
ISBN 0-8037-0794-0
ISBN 0-8037-0795-9 (lib. bdg.)

The art for this book was prepared by using watercolor over wood.
It was then camera-separated and reproduced in red, yellow, blue, and black.

Baby's Book
of Lullabies
&Radle Songs

selected and illustrated by

Yvonne Gilbert

DIAL BOOKS FOR YOUNG READERS
New York

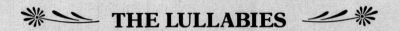

THE LULLABIES

1. **ROCK-A-BYE BABY**
   English

2. **LITTLE RED BIRD**
   Manx

3. **AN IROQUOIS LULLABY**
   Canadian

4. **CRADLE SONG**
   German

5. **A BASQUE LULLABY**
   Spanish

6. **THE WHITE HEN'S CRADLE SONG**
   Belgian

7. **HUSH LITTLE BABBIE**
   Irish

8. **ONCE UPON A TIME**
   Yiddish

9. **A HUMOROUS LULLABY**
   Norwegian

10. **A WELSH LULLABY**
    Welsh

11. **BYE, BABY BUNTING**
    English

12. **CRONAN**
    Scottish

13. **HUSH LITTLE BABY**
    North American

14. **TYROLEAN CRADLE SONG**
    Austrian

15. **LITTLE SON, HUSH-A-BYE**
    French

16. **GOLDEN SLUMBERS**
    English

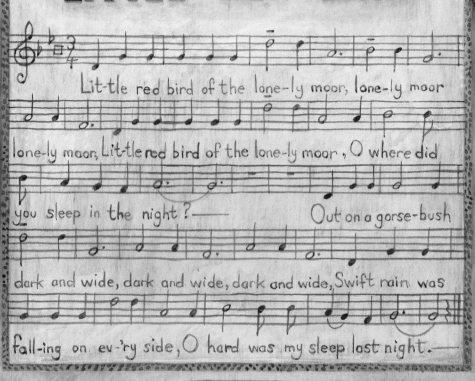

THE WHITE HEN'S CRADLE SONG

Hush Little Babbie

· BYE · BABY · BUNTING ·

CRONAN

Tyrolean Cradle Song

Little Son, Hush-a-Bye

Lit-tle son, hush-a-bye, bye. Dad-dy's far o'er the sea.—

Lit-tle son, hush-a-bye, bye. Mo-ther is watch-ing thee.—

Loud-ly the sea birds cry, cry. White waves are dash-ing high.—

Lit-tle son, hush-a-bye, bye. Mo-ther is watch-ing thee.

Golden Slumbers

✳ LYRICS ✳

1. ROCK-A-BYE BABY
English Traditional

Rock-a-bye baby, on the tree top,
When the wind blows the cradle will rock;
When the bough breaks the cradle will fall,
And down will come baby, cradle and all.

2. LITTLE RED BIRD

Little red bird of the lonely moor,
Lonely moor, lonely moor,
Little red bird of the lonely moor,
O where did you sleep in the night?

Out on a gorse-bush dark and wide,
Dark and wide, dark and wide,
Swift rain was falling on ev'ry side,
O hard was my sleep last night.

3. AN IROQUOIS LULLABY
English words by Alan Mills

Sleep, sleep, little one,
Sleep, sleep, little one,
Sleep, sleep, little one,
Now go to sleep, now go to sleep.

4. CRADLE SONG
By Brahms

Sink to slumber, good night,
Let thy dreaming be bright,
For lily and rose
Will guard thy repose
And when night time is past
May God wake thee at last,
And when night time is past
May God wake thee at last.

Sink to slumber, good night,
And angels of light
With love you shall fold
As the Christ-Child of old
While the stars dimly shine
May no sorrow be thine,
While the stars dimly shine
May no sorrow be thine.

✷ LYRICS ✷

5. A BASQUE LULLABY
By Florence Hoare

Lullaby, twilight is spreading
Silver wings over the sky;
Fairy elves are softly treading
Folding buds as they pass by;

Chorus:
Lullaby, whisper and sigh,
Lullaby, Lullaby!

Lullaby, daytime is weary,
Tired of work, tired of play;
Sleep, my baby, sleep, my dearie,
Now you are as tired as they,

Lullaby, deep in the clover
Drones the bee softly to rest;
Close, white lids, your dear eyes over,
Mother's arms shall be your nest.

6. THE WHITE HEN'S CRADLE SONG
Folk-tune

Hear the white hen calling,
In the farmyard calling.
"Cluck, cluck, cluck, Little chickens run
Underneath my wings each one,
Cheep! cheep! Close every eye now,
Cheep! cheep! Cosy you lie."

7. HUSH LITTLE BABBIE
By Winifred Ryan

Hush, little babbie, hush, go asleep.
Hush, little babbie, do not cry.
O then hush, little babbie, and go asleep,
For your mammy and daddy
Will be home by an' by.
With me ho hi hey hi ho

Where are you going, my old man?
Where are you going, my honey?
O then hush, little babbie, do not cry,
For your daddy and mammy
Will be home by an' by.
Musha ho hi hi ho hi ho
Ho ho hi ho di hill de ho ri am

✳ LYRICS ✳

8. ONCE UPON A TIME

Once upon a time there was,
Is the happy old beginning.
But our story's sad, and starts
With a Jewish King.

Chorus:
Hush my little birdie.
Hush my little baby.
I have lost my own true love.
Ah, woe is unto me.

The king he had a lovely queen,
The queen a vineyard fair had she.
The vineyard fair, it had a tree.
Hush my little baby.

On the tree there was a branch,
On the branch there was a nest,
In the nest there was a birdie,
Hush my little baby.

The king he died so suddenly,
The queen grew sad and pined away.
The branch broke off the tree, my love,
And the birdie flew away.

Where is there a wise man
Who can count the stars?
Where is there a doctor
Who can heal my heart?

9. A HUMOROUS LULLABY
Folk-tune.
English words by A. Forestier.

Birchrids booming, booming,
Pussy sets up a drumming,
And four small mice set to work to dance
Until the earth loudly thunders.

Tabby on the housetop
Called aloud to her daughters;
O what shall we in the winter do?
With frozen feet we will mew, mew.

10. A WELSH LULLABY
Traditional

Sleep my baby on my bosom,
Closely nestle safe and warm.
Mother wakeful watches o'er you,
Round you folded mother's arms.
Sweet, there's nothing near can hurt you,
Nothing threatens here your rest.
Sleep my baby, Sleep, and fear not,
Sleep you sweetly on my breast.

Lulla, Lulla, sweetly slumber,
Mother's treasure, slumber deep,
Lulla, Lulla, now you're smiling,
Smiling, dear one, through your sleep.
Say, are angels bending o'er you,
Smiling down from heaven above?
Is that heavenly smile your answer,
Love from dreamland answering love?

❋ LYRICS ❋

11. BYE, BABY BUNTING
Traditional

Bye, Baby Bunting,
Daddy's gone a hunting,
He's gone to fetch a rabbit skin
To wrap our Baby Bunting in.
Bye, Baby Bunting.

12. CRONAN
Translation by Lachlan Macbean.

Hush-a-bye, darling, and hush-a-bye, dear,
O, Hush-a-bye, darling will yet be a hero;
None will be bigger or braver or stronger,
Lullaby, little one, crying no longer.

Lullaby, little one, bonnie wee baby,
He'll be a hero and fight for us, maybe;
Cattle and horses and sheep will his prey be:
None will be bolder or braver than baby.

Softly and silently eyelids are closing;
Dearest wee jewel, so gently he's dozing;
Softly he's resting by slumber o'ertaken;
Soundly he's sleeping and sweetly he'll waken.

Placidly, peacefully, slumber has bound him;
Angels are lovingly watching around him—
Beautiful spirits, his sorrow beguiling,
Sweetly they whisper, and baby is smiling!

13. HUSH LITTLE BABY

Hush, little baby, don't say a word,
Mama's gonna buy you
A mockin' bird.

If that mockin' bird don't sing,
Mama's gonna buy you
A diamond ring.

If that diamond ring turns brass,
Mama's gonna buy you
A lookin' glass.

If that lookin' glass gets broke,
Mama's gonna buy you
A billy-goat.

If that billy-goat won't pull,
Mama's gonna buy you
A cart and bull.

If that cart and bull turn over,
Mama's gonna buy you
A dog named Rover.

If that dog named Rover don't bark,
Mama's gonna buy you
A horse and cart.

If that horse and cart fall down,
You'll be the sweetest
Little girl in town.

❋ LYRICS ❋

14. TYROLEAN CRADLE SONG

O hush thee, o hush thee,
My baby so small.
The ass has his crib
And the ox has his stall.
They shield thee, baby
From heaven above,
O hush thee, O hush thee,
My baby my love.

O hush thee, O hush thee,
My baby so small.
Dim is the light
From the lamp on the wall.
Bright in the night sky
There shineth a star,
Leading the kings
Who come from afar.

O hush thee, O hush thee,
My baby so small.
Joseph is spreading
The straw in the hall.
Soon you will sleep
In the nook of my arm,
Safe from all trouble
And danger and harm.

15. LITTLE SON, HUSH-A-BYE
Folk-tune

Little son, hush-a-bye, bye.
Daddy's far o'er the sea.
Little son, hush-a-bye, bye.
Mother is watching thee.
Loudly the sea birds cry, cry.
White waves are dashing high.
Little son, hush-a-bye, bye.
Mother is watching thee.

16. GOLDEN SLUMBERS
Traditional

Golden slumbers kiss your eyes
Smiles awake you when you rise;
Sleep, pretty darlings, do not cry,
And I will sing a lullaby.

Care you know not, therefore sleep,
While I o'er you watch do keep;
Sleep, pretty darlings, do not cry,
And I will sing a lullaby.

✳ ABOUT THE ILLUSTRATOR ✳

Yvonne Gilbert has illustrated a number of books including *Abbey Lubbers, Banshees, and Bogards (A Dictionary of Fairies)* by Catherine Briggs, and *The Iron Wolf* by Richard Adams. As well as illustrating books, Ms. Gilbert has illustrated stamps and has twice won awards for them—The Golden Stamp Award and The World's Most Beautiful Stamp. Her work has been widely exhibited both in England and the United States. Her young son Tom, who always liked being sung to sleep, was the inspiration for *Baby's Book of Lullabies and Cradle Songs*. He and some of his toys were the models for many of the pictures in the book, along with several of his friends and relatives. Ms. Gilbert lives with her husband and son in Newcastle-upon-Tyne, England.

The music in this book is based on original scores collected from many countries and written during different periods, leading to variations in style of notation. All the songs, however, are still accessible to the modern reader and music lover.